Volume 3: Crossroads

Story by
Marv Wolfman

Written by
Len Wein

Illustrated by
Wilson Tortosa

Contents

Steck
Vaughn™

A Harcourt Achieve Imprint

www.Steck-Vaughn.com
1-800-531-5015

ALL ABOARD!

Previously...

As the ten castaways journey across the Pacific Ocean, another storm causes the group to seek refuge in the perilous hills of the island chain. As the group treks inland, Amira loses her footing on the side of a cliff. She plummets toward the bottom of the hill, severely injuring her leg. Amira is unable to walk, but John and the others get Amira to safety.

Meanwhile, Eduardo and Eugene begin to disagree on the best plan for getting home. Eugene believes that the group will be discovered if they head for the beach while Eduardo demands the group press on to the other side of the island.

"I get what I want when I want it!"
—*Amira Albertson, 16*

"Whatever you say."
— *Layla Catava, 15*

"Follow me...I know the way."
— *Eugene Davis, 15*

"I need to work on my jump shot."
— *Eduardo Trejo, 17*

CHAPTER ONE

Several days have passed since the ten teens were washed ashore on this seemingly deserted South Pacific island. Each day has been filled with danger, fear, mystery...and conflict.

The castaways don't really know each other...who to trust, who to rely on.

Unless we want to spend the rest of our lives on this island, we have to make a choice.

7

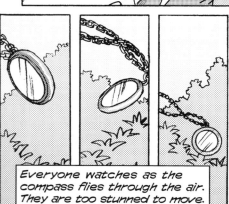

Everyone watches as the compass flies through the air. They are too stunned to move.

You can't blame this on me! If John wasn't so selfish, this wouldn't have happened!

Selfish? This isn't my fault!

Knock it off. We'll just have to travel without a compass.

Amira, you can lean on me if it's too difficult for you to walk.

We're heading this way. Good luck, Eduardo.

Each group disappears into the jungle, but not every member is sure that splitting up is the best thing to do.

Meanwhile, a mysterious figure lurks in the shadows.

9

Later...

Anne, you don't need to keep marking a trail behind us.

What if there *is* someone on this island? If they see our trail, maybe they'll follow it and rescue us.

You're just wasting your time. The only place anyone's going to rescue us is on the beach.

Well, it's my time to waste. At least I'm doing something.

Fine.

Besides, do you even know where we're going?

It would be easier with the compass, but if we watch the sun's position, we should be OK.

Aren't you afraid we're getting deeper into something we may not be able get out of?

Yes, that's why we have to stick together.

What's left of the group, anyway.

In spite of their fears, the group struggles to remain positive in the face of danger.

Meanwhile, on another part of the island...

Be careful, Amira. Try not to put too much weight on your leg.

When did you turn into my father? I can take care of myself!

I know you can, but you need my help. You won't make it very far on your own.

I'm sorry. Eduardo. I'm just not used to relying on other people.

AHHHHH

12

The other group has entered a small grove of fruit trees. They decide to take a break.

Whatever this stuff is, it tastes great!

At least we won't starve!

I just hope that nothing eats us.

WHOOOOOO

I know it's silly, but I really think the legend is true.

Yeah, I'm starting to believe it, too. But why are these islands haunted by ancient warriors?

ENOUGH! I refuse to believe in ghosts!

WHOOOOOO

Really? Maybe you should tell that to them.

I never believed in ghosts, but now I'm not so sure.

I'm sorry we split up with the others. I'd feel safer with more people around me.

We'd all feel safer, but Eduardo wouldn't listen. I guess there's nothing we can do about it now.

Our best chance is to get to the beach and somehow signal the rescue party.

WHOOOOOO

Meanwhile, the trek is becoming more difficult for Eduardo's group. Amira's injured leg is slowing them down, and tensions are beginning to rise.

How are you holding up, Amira?

Don't worry about me. I'm doing...

...AHHH!

AMIRA!

Your leg doesn't look good. It's really swollen.

Just let me rest a minute. I'll be fine.

We'll never get anywhere dragging you along.

Miri's right. I'm holding everyone back.

Look, why don't I just rest here for a while? You can go on without me and come back for me later.

NO! We got in this together, and we're getting out the same way!

But she said—

I don't care what she said. We're not leaving anyone behind. Pei, get on the other side of Amira and help her walk.

What makes you think you can order me around? If my dad was here—

Well, your daddy isn't here. You don't have a choice.

Whatever.

Are you sure we can make it?

Yes... you're coming with us.

17

Meanwhile, Eugene's group climbs higher and higher up the mountain. Anne continues to mark a trail behind them.

The path is so narrow. Is there another way we can go?

I don't see one.

Here...I'll hold on to one end of the oa and we'll walk acros together. It will hel us stay balanced.

OK... I guess.

Just take it one step at a time.

Keep your eyes open, and be careful.

The sun's behind us, so we're definitely going in the right direction for...

Whoa!

AHHHHHH!

For several terrifying seconds, John struggles to regain his balance.

Easy! I've got you!

That was close!

I'm sorry. I wasn't paying attention!

Good thing Eugene is here, or you'd be in pretty bad shape right now.

I'm so clumsy. Why can't I shape up?

Meanwhile, Eduardo's group is forced to make another decision.

Great! Now which way do we go?

Let's try that path. It seems a little wider.

Why not?

Yeah, what difference does it make?

I don't really know which path is the best one to take, but...

I say let's take the one to the right.

I'm getting tired. I'm not sure how much further I can go.

WHOOOOOOO

The wind is picking up.

Remember, Cai...you don't believe in ghosts.

WHOOOOOO

Unhhhh! The wind is too strong!

WHOOOOOO

I don't think we can make it through this path! We'll have to turn back and try the other path.

WHOOOOOO

...as they begin to head back the opposite direction...

Hey, the wind stopped!

So did the howling. It's like we were being warned not to take the other path.

Maybe it's not a ghost. Maybe someone's looking for us.

Well, if someone is out there looking for us, I wish they would tell us what to do. Watch out! You don't need another injury.

Eugene's group must avoid its own set of obstacles as the five teens make their way down the side of a cliff.

Come on, Layla, it's not that far. Once you're across, we'll help the others.

You know, Anne... I thought it was useless to carry that oar all this way, but I guess it has come in handy.

Eugene's a really nice guy. We couldn't have made it this far without him.

I'm just glad we didn't decide to use the oar for firewood or something.

eir initial shock turns into relief.

HA HA HA HA HA HA HA

I can't believe it! You should've seen your face!

My face? What about *your* face!

HA HA HA HA HA HA

HA HA HA HA HA

HA HA HA HA HA HA HA HA HA HA HA HA

The stress of the past several hours is soothed by their uncontrollable laughter.

WHOA!

The group's quick thinking prevents a tragedy.

Grab my hand! Hold on. We've got you.

Pull him back up!

Pei breathes a sigh of relief as the others pull him from the quicksand, but he has a hard time showing his gratitude.

Uhh... th-thanks.

It's all right, but you have to be more careful.

Watch your step, Miri.

Believe me, I'm watching every step I take.

Once Amira is lowered safely to the ground, the others climb down the cliff.

OK, let's keep going. Everyone's safe.

No thanks to me.

Don't be so hard on yourself, John. Amira is fine. We were all struggling to hang on to the vine.

But I lost control. Amira could have been hurt...or worse.

John, you've helped out a lot. She wouldn't have made it this far without you.

Whoa!

What is it?

I guess this island *is* inhabited after all!

at's he ?ing?

He's not moving. Why doesn't he say something?

Do you think he's dangerous?

How am I supposed to know?

Calm down. He doesn't want to harm us.

Maybe he can help us.

Why don't you try talking to him?

OK... I guess I'll try.

33

Hello. My name's Eugene. I'm sorry to bother you, but my friends and I are lost. We were wondering if you might be able to help us.

He's not responding. He didn't even blink.

He probably doesn't speak English.

Does anyone else want to try?

Several of the teens try to speak to the old man in Spanish, Chinese French, and other languages. The islander, however, doesn't respon

Suddenly...

Huh?

What is he doing?

He's going to attack us!

Easy, John... I don't think that's what he wants to do.

Look, he's drawing something.

What if he's trying to put some kind of spell on us or something. I read an article once—

Oh, come on, Anne. No, I don't think that's what he's doing.

I think he's trying to tell us something.

He's drawing fire. Maybe it's some kind of story.

Or maybe it's just a picture...you know, like a design.

No, I don't think so.

I think... I don't know... yes, I get it now!

Do you remember when the cruise director was telling us about the haunted islands?

Sort of... he said ancient warriors with incredible powers ruled these islands.

The warriors were heroic. They protected one another and helped those in need.

37

Anne reminds them that the warriors had the ability to control fire.

That's right! The cruise director said the fire warriors moved from island to island, helping other members of their tribe.

They punished those who tried to harm others. At least that's what the cruise director said.

This *does* sound a little familiar.

You're right! He's trying to tell us the same story the cruise director told us!

Wait. Why did he stop drawing?

This can't be the end of the story. There must be more...something we didn't hear the cruise director say after we left in the boat.

What's he doing now?

Why doesn't he finish the story?

Be careful. We don't know what he'll do next.

I'm pretty sure he's not going to hurt us.

Diego's right.

What's he doing with all those sticks?

I think he's building a fire.

Maybe he can teach us how.

Do you think he's a fire warrior, too?

If he is, he's a lot older than he looks.

Then again...he looks pretty old to me.

Diego, Anne...it's really cool how you guys made the connect between the drawings and the st the cruise director told us.

I guess all the drawing and reading we do is worth something after all...huh, Diego?

Yeah, I guess so.

The sun is going down.

Look...

...He's drawing again.

Most of the group eventually falls sound asleep...

...But Anne and Diego watch intently as the islander continues to draw.

Finally, even Diego and Anne are too exhausted to stay awake. As the group rests peacefully, the only sounds that are heard are the whispering wind, the crackling of the fire, and the scratching of a stick in the sand.

42

The old islander, the re...everything is gone!

It's as if he was never here!

There's no wood or ash anywhere.

What happened?

Maybe he was a—

Don't say what I think you're about to say!

A ghost.

I...I can't believe it!

Take a look at this!

Nothing on these islands makes sense to me.

Let's check this place out. Maybe we'll find something we can use.

I'll stay here, OK? I mean...just in case someone comes for us.

I'll stay here, too. My leg hurts. Do you think the islander was a ghost?

I don't know. I don't think I want to know.

Well, this was a waste of time.

Cai's right. There's nothing here but a bunch of old rocks.

Wait! That building's still standing.

Let's get a closer look.

45

These islands... everything is so strange!

Well, we could get out of here sooner if you'd walk a little faster!

I don't think we're going anywhere.

Terrific.

The river empties into a swamp.

How are we going to get past that?

Is there any way around it?

It doesn't look like it.

We'll never get off this island!

As they stare into the vastness of the swamp, the group suspects that Layla may be right. Their hopes begin to fade...

47

...But some refuse to give up.

We'll get home. It's just a matter of time. I know we're going to be rescued.

Yeah, but what shape will we be in when the search party does find us?

We'll be OK as long as we stay together. Let's—*HEY!* My foot!

Are you OK?

I'm fine, but I lost my shoe.

Be careful where you walk. It isn't quicksand, but it's just as dangerous.

No way I'm hiking through that stuff.

We have to. It's the only way out of here.

48

The group moves cautiously into the swamp.

I'll go first. Follow me.

I've got a **sinking feeling** there could be more quicksand around here.

Very funny, Cai.

Uhhh!

John, are you all right?

I'm fine.

49

Everyone! Grab onto the person next to you, and don't let go...no matter what!

Don't worry, Amira. I have you.

Hang on, Anne!

Oh, please let us make it through this!

I promise I won't let go, Cai.

Good to know.

Can you swim, Layla?

I guess I'm about to find out!

Brace yourselves!

The towering wave hits them like a wall, sweeping up everything and everyone in its path.

AAAAAAAAHHH!

Are you two OK?

I'm still breathing, if that's what you mean.

Yeah... I think I'm OK.

We have to get to higher ground! Hang on!

Here we go...

I don't see them!

No! They can't be...!

After all we've been through, I can't believe—

Wait! I see something!

It's them!

But something's wrong with Pei! He's not moving!

Come on, John! We're right here! You can make it!

I can't! I'm too tired! I...can't keep... fighting!

We have to help them!

How? They're too far away!

56

The teens hold onto one another
they pull John to safety.

Don't let go, Eugene!

I won't let him go.

John... give me your hand!

You're too far away!

Wait! The oar! Anne, use your oar to pull him up!

G-got it!

Uhhhhhh...

Later...

How are you feeling, Pei?

Like I was hit on the head with a baseball or something. How did I get here?

You were out cold and going under the water. John held onto you and kept you afloat until we could rescue both of you.

John, you... you saved my life.

It was nothing.

Thank you, John!

Really! It wasn't a big deal.

Yeah... it was!

Is this really Pei or just someone who looks like him?

John risked his own life to help another, and Pei recognizes this act of courage.

I don't know how to thank you, John.

Later, Eugene and John build a fire. The group begins to dry off.

Why is Pei by himself?

Pei, what are you doing?

I just want to finish this before the sun sets.

Finish what?

I'm using these stones to show rescuers which way we're headed...

...kind of like you were doing with your oar. I thought it was a good idea. Listen, Anne...I'm sorry for the way I treated you—

It's OK, Pei. Now come back to the fire.

The group hopes that the night will be as peaceful as the last...especially after all they've been through.

60

Meanwhile, on the Tempest...

The stranded teens have not been forgotten. Pei's father—Wu Lee—has powerful connections. He uses his influence to get extra helicopters that will aid in the search effort.

Come on! We're wasting time! My son is missing!

My son is missing, too! Yelling won't help us.

Let's all try to keep calm. Otherwise, we're not doing our children any good.

PUCKAPUCKAPUCKA

Thank you, Mr. Lee, for everything! We'd never find our children without these helicopters!

I'll spend any amount of money! Whatever it takes to find Pei.

PUCKAPUCKAPUCKA

All the parents join in the search.

I'm afraid of flying! I think I might be sick...

You're OK, Jean. I know how much you care for Anne. We'll get through this.

If Diego had listened to me more often instead of drawing pictures, he would be safe.

I didn't spend enough time with John. I promise to make up for that. I hope we find them soon.

I hope so, too, but I have to remember...we may never see them again.

I hope Amira is OK. I'm frightened, Mia.

Let's hope they're all together...looking out for each other.

Mrs. Albertson is right. They are all intelligent. They know what to do.

A few remain hopeful, but tension threatens to divide the parents.

The teens, however, have been strengthened by their ordeal.

We work together from now on...not against each other...what do you say?

I agree.

Me, too.

Wait a second. John?

John, get over here.

I've never made friends very easily, but I guess these guys are OK.

Count me in. We're in this together.

OK. No more splitting up. No more going off on our own.

Everyone will have a chance to speak up. When we're not sure what we should do, we'll take a vote.

We have to be fair to each other.

Sounds good. So how about we start looking for some food? Anyone want to come with me?

Sure. I'm starving—

WHOOOOOOO

WHOOOOOOO

That shadow... it's coming closer!

To be continue